MYRTLE the HURDLER
and HER PINK and PURPLE, POLKA-DOTTED GIRDLE

Marybeth Dillon-Butler

Written by Marybeth Dillon-Butler
Illustrated by David Messing

First Page Publications

12103 Merriman • Livonia • MI • 48150
1-800-343-3034 • Fax 734-525-4420
www.firstpagepublications.com

Library of Congress Control Number: 2005901835
MYRTLE the HURDLER and HER PINK and PURPLE, POLKA-DOTTED GIRDLE/Marybeth Dillon-Butler
ISBN # 1-928623-23-9

Summary: Myrtle the Hurdler is a leisure-loving turtle whose poor eating habits prompt her to wear a girdle to firm up her middle. In preparation for a big track meet, Myrtle cuts back on junk food, eats more fruits and vegetables, and begins working out. Her efforts pay off when she becomes fit and wins the hundred-meter hurdle race.

First Page Publications
12103 Merriman Road
Livonia, MI 48150

Marybeth Dillon-Butler:

This book is dedicated to my brother John—the bravest, kindest, funniest, strongest hurdler I've ever known; to my wonderful parents Jan and Jack, who instilled in me the love of reading; and to my husband Patrick, and children Maureen and Sean, who share that love. Special thanks go to illustrator David Messing, all the folks at First Page Publications, and artists Maureen Butler and Jack Dillon.

Dave Messing:

I know, firsthand, how Myrtle felt when she looked into the mirror, saw her tummy, and thought . . . "WOW, is that me?"

When I was seven and eight years old, I was the heaviest kid on the playground! One summer day, my mother told me that she would help me change my diet. She knew I loved candy, so she said that if I ate all the good and healthy foods, she would reward me with one candy bar every day. It took a little getting used to, but after a week or so, I developed a taste for healthy foods like celery and cottage cheese instead of ice cream topped with caramel . . . topped with whipped cream . . . topped with nuts.

A few more weeks passed and I remember "banking" a candy bar for the next day, because I just wasn't in the mood for sweets! From then on, the more weight I lost, the more I played and exercised. By the end of the summer, I had lost a lot of my weight and needed new school clothes. One of my fondest grade-school memories was that first day back from summer vacation when my friends and classmates couldn't believe it was me.

So I would like to dedicate this book to every kid who looks in the mirror and decides that he or she is going to eat right, exercise, and be healthy!

Eat right for a good, long life.

Love,
Myrtle

Myrtle the Turtle
lived near the water
with Big Sister Nellie,
Mother and Father.

She played on the beach
and lounged on her log.
Every once in a while,
she went for a joy.
But mostly she feasted
on treats in the bog.

She munched so much she had a bit of a belly.
It grew flappy and floppy, and jiggled like jelly . . .
'til one day she moaned to Big Sister Nellie,
"I've got to do something to tone up these muscles.
The track meet is coming. I've got to hustle!"

Myrtle the Turtle and some of her pals
ran track and cross country at a school for gals.
There were Myrtle and Mabel, Toni and Amy.
Head of the team was the great Coach Davey.

Father Turtle loved Myrtle.
He fretted and stewed over his dear daughter's middle.
"It's my fault," he said. "All those cakes from my griddle!"

Mother said, "Here's an idea I'd like to propose:
Hold in your stomach, so it won't be exposed.

"With your shoulders
pulled back and your
posture erect, maybe
no one will notice your
tummy's unchecked!"

"I've tried that,"
sighed Myrtle. "But you
can't hide neglect."

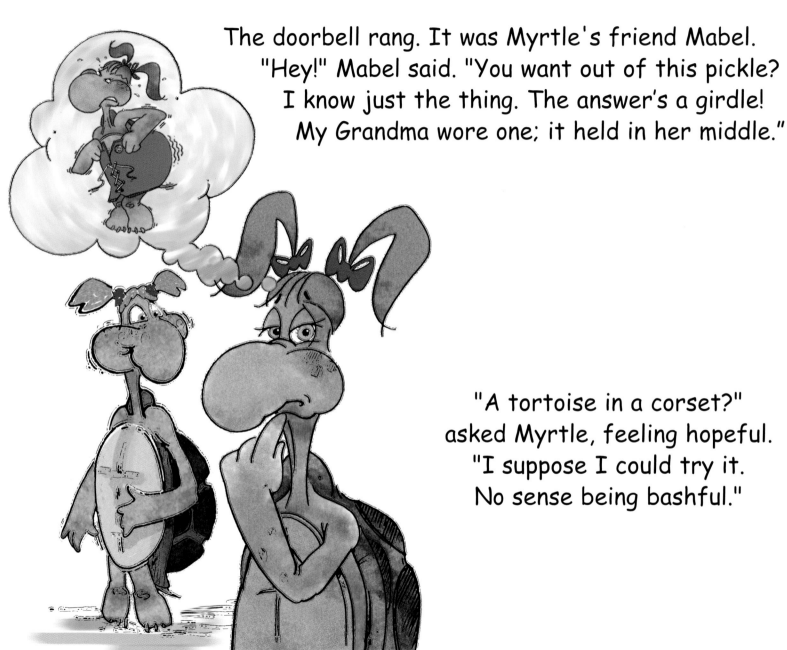

The doorbell rang. It was Myrtle's friend Mabel.
"Hey!" Mabel said. "You want out of this pickle?
I know just the thing. The answer's a girdle!
My Grandma wore one; it held in her middle."

"A tortoise in a corset?"
asked Myrtle, feeling hopeful.
"I suppose I could try it.
No sense being bashful."

To the mall went the girls, looking for girdles.
They found one on sale—just perfect for turtles.

Myrtle was tickled.
She looked fit as a fiddle
in a pink and purple,
polka-dotted
girdle.

Myrtle wore her corset both day and night.
Only thing was, it didn't feel quite right.
Too bad girdles had to be laced so tight!

When spring break came, it was time to swim and play.
But the girdle Myrtle wore kept getting in the way.
She'd take it off now and then—just to breathe a little.
But sadly for Myrtle, she still had her middle.

Only two months remained 'til the big competition.
Myrtle started training for her serious mission.
"I need Myrtle to run the hundred-meter hurdles,"
came word from Coach Davey, the number-one turtle.

To track practice she went, right after school.
Myrtle ran hundreds and four-hundreds too—
whatever Coach Davey asked her to do.
The harder she trained, the more fit she grew.
Myrtle cut back on candy and ate more fruit.

Veggies tasted better than ever before.
Myrtle felt stronger. She had pep galore!

The big day arrived.
The track meet was here!
Busloads of runners came
from schools far and near.
Fans packed the stands.
Families came to cheer.

Myrtle looked peachy warming up
near the blocks,
ready to race in spikes
and pink socks.

Other competitors looked
pretty cool, too.
Jan wore new racing flats;
Ann spikes of blue.
Said Coach to his team,
"Run *all* the way through!"

"*Take your marks*!" yelled the starter. "*Get set. Go*!"
With the blast of a gun came the start of the show.
Over the hurdles jumped Myrtle, Jan and Jo.

Nipping their heels were Kit, Ann and Bridget,
all trained to fly—and visibly fit!

Trouble brewed for Myrtle
from the very first inch.
"Oh no!" gasped Myrtle,
as the darn girdle pinched.

Myrtle was worried
and losing ground fast.
No way, no how
did she want to be last!

Ann, Jo and Kit were passing her now.
Myrtle was moving, but slow as a cow.
As she neared the fourth hurdle, something went POW!
What in the world was happening now?

With all of that straining,
her laces came loose.
Myrtle's girdle popped off.

It flew like a goose!

"Oh my!" cried Myrtle,
sailing over a hurdle.
Coach Davey shouted,
"Keep pushing, Myrtle!"

She pumped her arms and
tried to run faster.
Her legs and lungs hurt.
Was she courting disaster?

Near the sixth hurdle,
Myrtle passed Jan.
She gave it her all.
It worked! She passed Ann!

With two hurdles to go,
Kit had the lead.
Her foot hit a hurdle.
She was losing her speed.

It was Myrtle and Jo, in a dead heat for first.
With one hurdle left, Myrtle needed a burst.
She said to herself, "I'll make one final push."

Like lightning she ran, feet barely touching the ground.
After all that hard training, she'd lost five pounds!

Myrtle lunged at the finish, and to her surprise,
by a nose, she beat Jo!

She won first prize!

Soon she was greeted with the happiest cries.

"Bravo!" called Coach, handing Myrtle her medal.
"Fantastic!" gushed Father. "You did it!" praised Mabel.

"I'm so proud," beamed Mother.
"Group hug!" cried Sister.

"Oh, thank you," said Myrtle, "but I owe it to you.
I just can't imagine a better support crew."

"You know what?" asked Myrtle, giving Mabel high five.
"Turtles with tummies can do without girdles.
All they need is *exercise*.
Work out and eat smart. You'll be just the right size!"

Myrtle felt happy, so strong and so proud—
she smiled 'til her dimples showed. . . laughing out loud.
It seemed she was floating on her own special cloud.

Marybeth Dillon-Butler

A journalism graduate of the University of Michigan, Marybeth is a freelance writer and marathoner who previously worked as an award-winning newspaper editor and reporter. She co-authored *A History of the Incorporated Society of Irish/American Lawyers*, and is one of just four non-lawyers to be named an honorary member of the Society. A silver medalist in the 1996 Irish Olympic Marathon Trials, Marybeth lives in southeastern Michigan with her husband Patrick, children Maureen and Sean, and a red fish named Firefighter.

David Messing

After graduating from Wayne State University in Detroit, Michigan with a split major of advertising design and sculpture, Dave started cartooning for youth-oriented magazines. Dave, his wife Sandy, and their boys Scott, Kevin and Adam have taught in their family-owned art school, Art 101, for twenty-five years. Dave also designs and builds props and miniatures for film and print commercials. You have seen his work on T.V. and billboards and in national magazines and movies. His client list ranges from historical museums to Harley-Davidson to almost every car manufacturer. He enjoys teaching and all forms of art, from sculpture to cartooning.